STAR WARS™ ADVENTURES

THE WEAPON OF A JEDI

STAR WARS™ ADVENTURES

THE WEAPON OF A JEDI

BASED ON THE NOVEL BY JASON FRY

ADAPTATION BY ALEC WORLEY

ART BY RUAIRÍ COLEMAN

COLORS BY CHRIS O'HALLORAN

LETTERS BY AMAURI OSORIO
AND 49 GRAD-MEDIENAGENTUR

COVER ART BY RUAIRÍ COLEMAN

I think that was the last of those *TIE fighters, Luke.*
No. Keep your eyes peeled, Wedge. We got another one hiding out here somewhere.
I got nothing on my scanners, buddy. How do you know?
I just *know.*
THE WEAPON OF A JEDI
PYOSSSSSSSSHH!
RRRRRRRGGGGHHHHHH!
PYOOOOW!
VREEEEEET!
PYOOOOW!

The space lanes above the planet Giju.
WAH-REEEEP!
That was *not* too close, Artoo!
Woooop! Woooop! Beeda-bleeep!
You keep the fighter flying. Let me worry about what to do with it.
KROOOOOM!

Luke, how did you...? Ah, never mind.

You know, for just an hour, I'd like to know what it's like to fly with *the Force* watching *my* back.

It's almost as good as having you watching my back, Wedge.
Nice flying, gentlemen...

Looks like we bought our transport enough time to get clear of the Imperials and calculate the jump into hyperspace.
Okay, Red Squadron. We're done here...

Activate your *scatter protocols*. Let's make it nice and hard for any patrols thinking of tracking us.
We'll meet at the rendezvous point at 2300 hours.
Copy that, boss. See you guys on the other side.
Access the jump pattern for the planet Devaron, Artoo.

Then I need you to...
Huh...?

Bweeda-whooo?
I'm fine, pal. Honest. I just had a weird feeling, like there was something in my mind, like a... a word I couldn't quite remember.
I think the Force is trying to *tell* me something.
Boy, I wish Ben was here. What's the good of knowing *the Force* with no one left to teach me how to use it?
Artoo, can you take the stick? I want to try meditating while we're in hyperspace. Maybe that will help me figure out what's going on.

I need to relax. Empty my mind.
What was it Ben said? "Only by emptying your mind will the Force be able to fill it."
Let go of your emotions... Let yourself drift...
It... It's working! I can see something...
"I'm in another *time*... A time yet to come... In a place I've yet to visit...
"*Training remotes!* Like the one Han kept for blaster practice aboard the *Millennium Falcon*.
"I had enough trouble deflecting the blasts of just *one* of these things, but *three*?
"The Force is *strong* in this place. I can feel it all around me, a living thing, like wind or rain.
"But there's something else here. Something *dark* lurking nearby.
Something..."

Tweeeet! Bdeep-wooop?
I'm... I'm okay, Artoo.
It was the Force. It was showing me some kind of vision. But I've got no idea what it means.
Guess I'll just have to keep my mind open and hope the next thing it shows me is easier to understand.
Anyway, looks like Commander Narra and Wedge beat us to the refuelling station...
Sorry I'm late.
Just in time for your latest orders, Lieutenant Skywalker.
Mon Mothma's asked you to retrieve Imperial communication logs intercepted by rebel cells along the Shipwright's Trace.
Yeah, I know it's boring work, but those logs could give us a picture of Imperial operations on the entire trade route.
Think of it as your chance to get out there and see the galaxy.
The mission details have been loaded into your astromech. He's on his way to Docking Bay 12 to do preflight on your Y-wing.
You'll be flying Y4, one of the two-seat models.
A two-seater? Is someone from the Alliance coming with me?

They certainly are. I believe you already know C-3PO...
I don't know why this is so difficult for you to process. As a translator, my skills are *essential* to the success of this mission.
That means a weekly oil bath is *well* within allowable regulations, and the *quality* of the lubricant used is *critically* important.
I believe the oil you have on board might date back to the First Coruscani Migration. If it got any *sludgier,* it would actually be solid.

Good luck, Skywalker.
Yeah, Luke. Enjoy that brick of a ship you'll be flying!

And watch out for Imperial patrols.
Devaron's lightly garrisoned, but it's not too far from Giju. We just embarrassed the Empire so I wouldn't be surprised if they threw a dragnet over this *entire* region.

So nice to see you again, Master Luke.
I've prepared a dossier for each of our *three* stops on this mission. I'm particularly excited to visit Whiforla II.
Whiforla-song is one of the six million forms of communication in which I am fluent, and among the most complex.

I can instruct you in the proper fluting for ceremonial introductions to the rebel leaders there, though as a human, your vocal range will limit you to basic greetings.
I'm afraid this will force us to cut the exchange of well wishes to less than an hour.
That *is* a shame. Now come on...

"...I've got to go change my clothes."
YOU THERE!
Halt!

Oh my! Stormtroopers. As dangerous fugitives, we'll surely be captured and sent to some terrible prison.
Easy, Threepio. There's no reason to suspect us of anything. Just remember our cover story.
Besides, I've picked up a few tricks watching Han bluff his way past Imperials. Just you watch.
Hand over your identification and explain your purpose here.
We're *hyperspace scouts*, just like it says right *here*.
We're refuelin' before we head out to the Western Reaches. Got a good tip on a Tibanna gas deposit. Interstellar gas-- the really pure stuff.

But don't go jumpin' my claim now.
We have no interest in wild rumors about space gas.

And what *exactly* does a hyperspace scout need with a *protocol droid?*
Oh, dear...

Oh, this one can talk to *anything*. He's programmed with about a million strange Wild Space dialects and old trade languages.
Plus, I've made a few special modifications. Even taught him to cook a not-bad pot of *chuba stew*.

No need for that look, sir! *Chubas* ain't just Hutt chow, you know. That's an unfortunate misconception.
You just need to *season* them with a touch of--
Yes, yes. Now carry on. *Please!*

And remember, it's the duty of *every* Imperial citizen to report suspicious activity. In *any* region.
Yes, sir!
Thank goodness.

I'm not programmed to resist interrogation.
Now perhaps we could start practicing the first of the four Whiforlan fluting forms.
Master Luke...?
Master Luke, what is it?
Sorry, Threepio. It's just that... I think I can hear something *calling* me.
It's coming from down *there*, from Devaron.
Maybe *that's* where the Force wants me to go? Maybe it's something to do with my vision.
I'm afraid I'm not sure what you're talking about, Master Luke.
But I *must* insist we get to our ship. I've compiled a detailed timetable that covers our *entire* schedule. I'll explain in more detail on the way.
I can't wait.

Vreet! Buur-Blaat!
I have *every* right to complain, Artoo.
Space travel used to be so much more *civilized*.

One could simply travel from place to place, rather than meandering about like a Purcassian river eel during spawning season.
Wouldn't you agree, Master Luke?
Sure.

Forgive me, Master Luke. But you do seem rather *preoccupied*. Is anything the matter?
Just that *feeling* I had back at the refueling station over Devaron.

I can't help thinking the Force was trying to tell me something.
Maybe I should be going to Devaron to find out *what*, instead of running errands in the far corners of the galaxy.

Maybe the Force was trying to stop me from making some kind of *mistake*.
Attention, unknown fighter!

This is the Imperial frigate *Kreuge's Revenge!*
The Tertiary Usaita system is *restricted*.
Shut down all flight systems and prepare for inspection!

What maniac charted our scatter program to bring us out *here?* We're *doomed!*
We were bound to run into a patrol at some point, Threepio! Artoo, calculate the next jump and get us *out* of here!

KRRRM!
BRRRRM!
Uhn!

RRRRRRRRRRRRRRRRGGHH!
How long until we can make jump to hyperspace, Artoo?
Tweet-Tweet! Bree-wrrp!
A *minute?*
Artoo, we're not going to last five ***seconds*** out here! Do something!

Bree-Vreet! Brrrt!
What do you mean you're triangulating our position? This isn't the time for stargazing, you miserable lump of circuits!
Threepio, keep it down!

I can't *concentrate*.

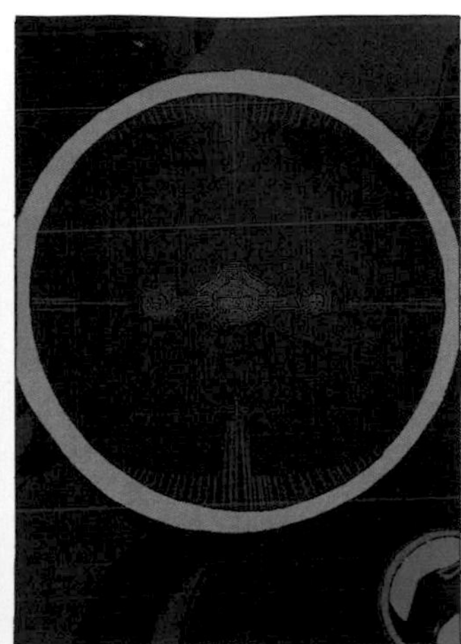

KROOOM!

Artoo, increase the power!
I can't outfly them in this junkpile. We'll have to tough it out instead!

Focus. Use *the Force.*

CLIK!

KROOOSH!
Well *done,* Master Luke!

Aaaah! I spoke too soon!

There goes our *starboard shield!*
If we can just hold on for another *30 seconds...*
BE-BE-BE-BE-BEEEP!

He's open.

His heart racing, Luke could feel his connection to the Force slipping.

I'm amazed he's lasted this long.
He's an *excellent* pilot, whoever he is.

Wouldn't you agree, *Lieutenant Pyparr?*
I didn't ask for an assessment of the scoundrel's abilities, Ensign.

I asked for him to be *destroyed!*

He keeps rolling, trying to cover that starboard engine...

Not for much longer.

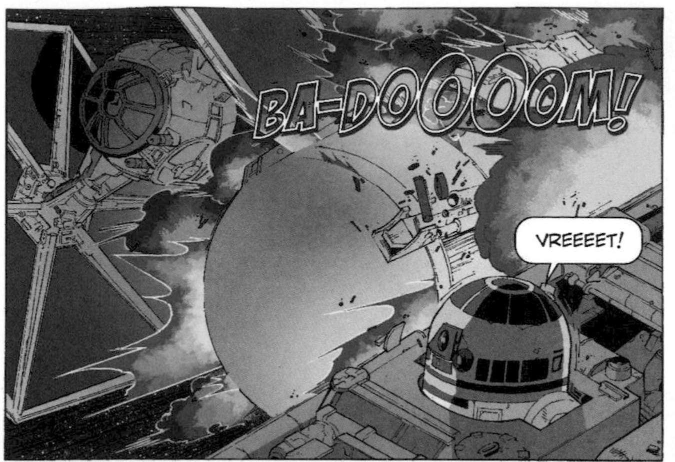
BA-DOOOOOM!
VREEEET!

Artoo, divert power! We got another 15 seconds...
If I can take down one more, we might be able to make it out of here...

Missed!
He's too fast!

Oh, my! This is the end!

I'm sorry, Ben... I tried my best...
WHOOP! WHOOP!

BWEE-DA TWEEET!
The jump calculations are *complete?*

Punch it, Artoo! Punch it now!

He's getting away! Take him down!
WWOOOOOOOSH!
Lost him!
Find that ship! Now!
He's badly damaged, Ensign. He'll be crawling for the nearest spaceport, no doubt...
"...We shall meet him again soon enough..."
Ba-deep? Bwee-oop?
No, Artoo. Those spaceports are either too far away or too tightly controlled by the Empire.
We... We're going back to Devaron.
But, Master Luke, our mission!

Send an encrypted message to the fleet. Tell them we'll resume the retrieval mission after we repair our fighter.

Breeep! Beeda-beep! Blarrt
No, Artoo!

My mind's made up...

"...Take us back to the planet *Devaron*. I need to know what's down there..."

Pirate trouble, huh?
Should probably *report* that to the *Imperial governor*.
If you give us your *name,* we can do the paperwork for you...
Name's *Korl Marcus.* I'm a *hyperspace scout.*

But really, my droids and I just need some *repairs*... Did I mention I have *credits?*

You must understand our suspicions.
My daughter *Farnay* and I get a lot of *unsavory* characters passing through.

The Empire doesn't pay too much attention to a backwater town like *Tikaroo.*
Anyway, let me fetch some tools and we'll take a proper look at your problem...

I can repair this with what I have in the shop. But it will take a few days.

And six thousand credits. All in advance.
Six thousand? Master L--I mean, *Korl*, this man does not run a reputable business. I suggest we--
That will *do*, Threepio.
VREEET?

It *would* cost *less* if I had replacement parts shipped in from the capital.
But then there'd be a lot of *paperwork*. Permits, bureaucrats asking questions, *that* sort of thing.
Oh, there's enough paperwork in the galaxy as it is.

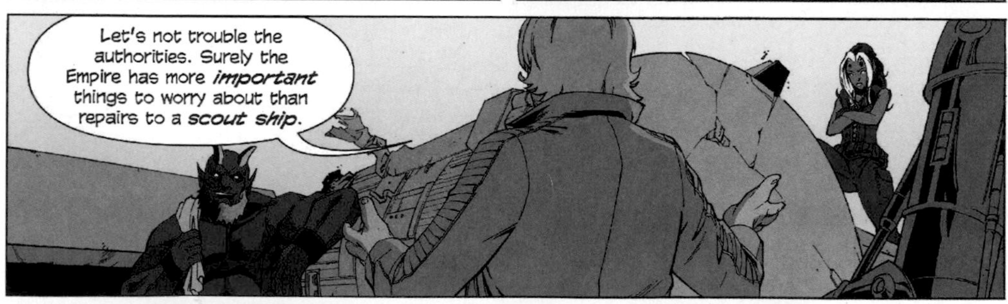
Let's not trouble the authorities. Surely the Empire has more *important* things to worry about than repairs to a *scout ship*.

I'll get your fighter under cover, then.
Town's *that* way...

"...I know a half-decent place where you can rent a room..."
That's the price of a room, outlander. If you don't like it, you can go sleep in the street.
Fine, I'll take the room.
Well, really!
Welcome to Tikaroo, my friend.
You look like a man in need of a native guide! Someone like me.
I've been exploring this jungle since I was a boy. I know every pool, sand pit, and shady glade the pikhrons like to visit.
Glad to hear it. But what's a pikhron?
My data file on this planet is basic, but apparently pikhrons are native herbivores.
Their skins and teeth fetch considerable prices on the black market, as hunting them is forbidden by Imperial decree.
I'm not much of a hunter, but I could sure use a guide.
I want to take a look at those ruins I saw in the jungle on my way in.

Was it something I said—
Whoa!
Oh, no!
VREEEEP!

The ruins of Eedit are off limits!
You'd bring disaster to us all, messing with that place. It would risk everything we have left.
Why? I don't understand.

All you need to know is to stay away, outlander!
I don't tolerate troublemakers, and you're already on my bad side.
Think I'll turn in then. Maybe we can make a fresh start tomorrow.

I know you're disappointed not to find a guide, Master Luke, but no doubt it's for the best.

I almost think I'd prefer getting shot at by the Empire to a suicidal trek into jungles prowled by savage beasts.
Well, I'm not afraid of jungle beasts or whatever superstition these locals might believe about those ruins.

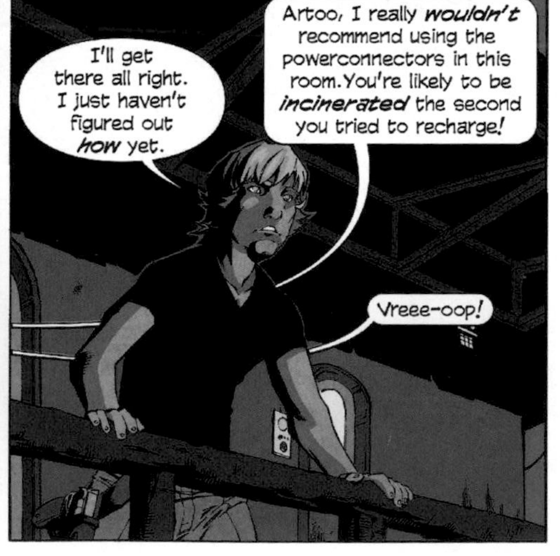
I'll get there all right. I just haven't figured out how yet.
Artoo, I really wouldn't recommend using the powerconnectors in this room. You're likely to be incinerated the second you tried to recharge!
Vreee-oop!

Uhnn...

AHH!
RREEEP?

I... I'm okay, Artoo.
I think I just had another dream...

"...I dreamed I was by a lake somewhere.
"Except... except it wasn't *me* who was there...

"...I was *someone else*.

"I could *feel* him kicking *down* into the water. It was so *peaceful* down there, so cool and quiet.

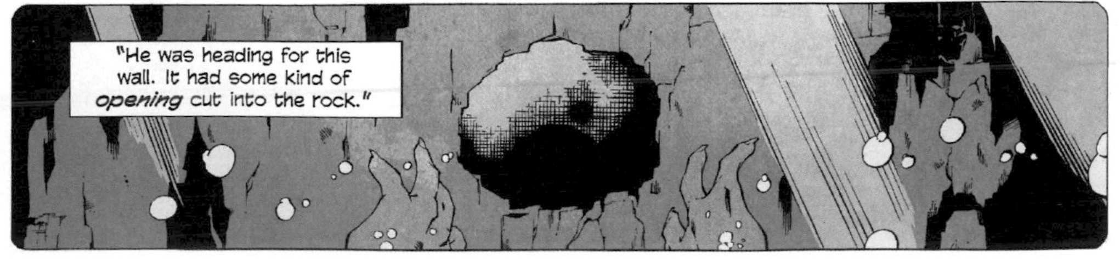
"He was heading for this wall. It had some kind of *opening* cut into the rock."

"Inside there was a stone staircase. He swam up and up.

"And when he reached the surface, there was someone *waiting* for him.

"Someone who gave him a *lightsaber*."

Those moons!
And the constellations. They're *identical* to ones I saw in my *dream!*
VRA-DEEET?

I was dreaming of *this place*, of *Devaron!*
The Force is giving me another clue about where to go!

There's a *lake* out there in the jungle, a lake visited by an alien Jedi long ago.
It's hiding a *secret passageway*, and tomorrow we're gonna *find* it, Artoo!
WEEEP! WEEEP! VOODA-DOOP!

VOOOT! DA-WEP? BIP-BIP?
I don't have enough command over the Force to get us through that jungle, Artoo.
And that *Imperial patrol* that hit us will be out there *looking* for us. So we need to leave as soon as the ship's repaired.
We'll just have to search the town for another *guide*. They can name their price.
Surely *one* of them is going to be greedy enough to risk a journey to those ruins.
Excuse me, Master Luke...

...I believe someone is *following* us.

I don't think you're cut out to be a spy, *Farnay*.
You just got caught by a *protocol droid*.

I... I trailed you to the depot last night and heard you asking about the towers, about Eedit. I could've warned you how they'd react.
You know about *Eedit?*
I sure do. I can take you there!
Follow me...

Later.
I've led hunting parties into the jungle *plenty* of times, and I can tell you there's *nothing* scary about Eedit.
It's just a bunch of ruins, but the *Empire* doesn't allow anyone to go there.

They say it was a temple for the sorcerers in the old war.
You mean the *Jedi?* Is *that* why the Empire forbids the guides from going there?

Well, that and the guides believe the place is *haunted* by the spirits of those who died there.
But I think they like telling that story better than admitting they're all afraid of *Porst*--he's the guy with the *eyepatch* who runs the depot.
He owns most of the equipment in Tikaroo, and if you cross him, he won't rent to you.

So here's my *pack beast*.
When do you want to get started?

MURRHHM?
I am not programmed for zoology, but this animal appears to be a *juvenile*.
He's a bit small, but he's *strong*.

TWEETA-TWOOOOP!
SCHLUURRPP!

I'm sure he's *very* strong, Farnay, but the two of us, plus my droids, would be too much for him to carry.

But all that information about Eedit has been really valuable. So let me give you a few credits for your time.
Huh?

A laser sword!

You touch that thing and I'll *blast* you!
Are you one of those *sorcerers*? Don't even *think* about trying to take over my brain! I've heard the stories, so don't try it!

VREEEEET!
Oh my goodness!

Famay, take it easy. I'm *not* a Jedi.
The lightsaber belonged to my father. He's dead. It's my only connection to him.

If you're not a sorcerer, then what *are* you? You're paying Dad a *crazy* amount of credits not to report your ship to the Empire.
Are you some kind of *rebel?*

Master Korl is a *hyperspace scout,* as he told your father. Don't you know it's rude to question your elders, young lady? To say nothing of pointing weapons at them.
It's all right, Threepio.
Now, Famay, put the gun down. I'll tell you the *truth*...

...My real name is *Luke Skywalker,* and I *am* a rebel--

--I'm fighting to restore freedom to the galaxy.
By getting rid of the Empire? But that's *impossible*.

Sometimes it *feels* that way, I *know*.
But people like me are working *together* on *thousands* of worlds to *resist* the Empire.
And on thousands of *other* worlds, people are realizing that the Empire's order comes at an enormous price--planets ruined and lives lost. All to feed the Emperor's *greed*.

Before the war with the droids, when my parents were young, people in this town were farmers.
They followed the *old ways*, living in harmony with the *forest elders*--that's what '*pikhron*' means in our language.
Then the *Empire* came.

When my mother *died* last year, I *had* to start leading pikhron hunts or we would have lost our *house*. Dad was so *angry* at me, but it doesn't matter now.
Woooo!
No one wants me as a guide anyway. You see, I've *never* bagged a pikhron, not that I ever *wanted* to.
But things will be *different* now, right? Here, in Tikaroo.
That's why the rebels sent you here, isn't it? To help us?

I wasn't *sent* here, Farnay. It's hard to explain, but I was... *called* to the temple.
My mission is *there*, not here.
But if you're patient, I *promise* I'll find a way to help Tikaroo. Somehow, what I find in the temple will show me how to do that.
I don't understand.
Neither do I. Not yet. But I *will*.

I do hope we find a guide *soon*. All this damp jungle air is making my joints rust.
Brreeep!

You there! You're *Marcus*, right? The outlander who wants to go on a pikhron hunt.
I'm not a hunter, but I want to hire a guide, yes. Are you available, Mr...?

Sarco Plank.

I'll take you into the jungle.
And unlike those *other* fools, *I don't* listen to tales about ghosts and sorcerers. I also have my own gear and mounts, and I can have them ready within *two hours*.
For the right price.

Master Luke, I'm not sure I like the *look* of this creature.
He doesn't feel right to *me* either, Threepio. But Farnay can't take us with just one half-grown pack beast.
Our only *other* option is to risk the journey on our own.
So, Marcus...

Do we have a *deal*...?

I guess we do.
Vweeep! Vweeep! Twoo-da-diiit!

Later.
Wait!

So it's *true*, then.
I didn't want to believe it! You're actually going into the woods with *the Scavenger*!

You *know* I don't like that name.
Or *kids* telling tales about me.

Tales about *what*? Your customers who don't come back, who wind up *robbed* and *murdered*?
What lie will it be *this* time, *Scavenger*?
Will you claim he fell off a cliff? Or maybe that he was gored by a pikhron bull?

Perhaps it would be better if Artoo and I stayed here and supervised repairs.
I'll be careful, Farnay.
Remember, I've got a trick or two up my sleeve.

So does *he*!

Time to go, Marcus.
GHHRRNNN.

Remember what I told you, Famay...

...and trust me.

I have a bad feeling about this.

Hours later.
Voota-voota!

Wooooo!
Peaceful? You're obviously malfunctioning.
I expect that any moment we'll be stomped to bits! Or bitten in two by some monstrous predator!

Or blown to bits because you won't shut up.
Wait!

Over there.
Pikhrons!

You have keen senses for an outlander.
If only you knew I can feel them through the Force.
I can sense they're calm, but... wary.

Here! Borrow my rifle. You can get a clear shot from here.

I'll pay you whatever you would have earned from the skins. But we're leaving the pikhrons *alone*.
And if you want to make some *more* easy credits, you can take me to *the ruins of Eedit!*

Forbidden.

What are you afraid of?
Nothing. But there's a difference between brave and *stupid*.
Then what's the danger? Look, I just want to *see* the place. I won't go inside. I'm... interested in old sites.

First you're a hyperspace scout, now you're some kind of *historian*?
Is *that* why you carry that antique laser sword?

I saw you *hiding* it inside your jacket when you climbed on board.
Uh, yes. Historical interest. That's all. I'm interested in relics and old sites.

Hmmm! So am *I*...
Very well, *Marcus*. I'll take you to see the ruins.
For an additional price, of course.

This is as far as I can take you, outlander.
You're right, Threepio! Those are definitely the towers we saw when we flew in.

Be careful! Those are Imperial sensors.
They form a perimeter around the whole of these ruins.
So there's no way in without being detected and bringing the Empire down on everyone in Tikaroo.

Tweeda-doo!
Artoo says he's willing to deactivate the sensors. Though that strikes me as reckless even by his standards.
You're right, Threepio. It's too risky. But I think I know another way into those ruins.

Take me to the lake. The one that's nearby.
There is no lake near here. Just the old dam destroyed in the droid war. It's just a dried-up riverbed now. There's nothing there.

A dam? Perhaps the water I had seen in my dream wasn't a lake at all, but an artificial reservoir?
This dam? is it outside the sensor barrier?
Yes, but...
Then that's where we're going!

You are full of surprises, outlander. Hhnn!
First you know of this dam...

...Then you know of a *cave* that would have been hidden below the waterline before the dam was destroyed.
How did you *know* all this?
Never mind how. We'll be inside for a few days at least. I'll raise you on the comlink when we're ready to return.

Like we agreed?
Like we agreed.
We'll meet again, Marcus. If you come out alive...

These steps lead straight into the Temple of Eedit. They're exactly what I saw in my vision.
This is what the Force wanted me to find.

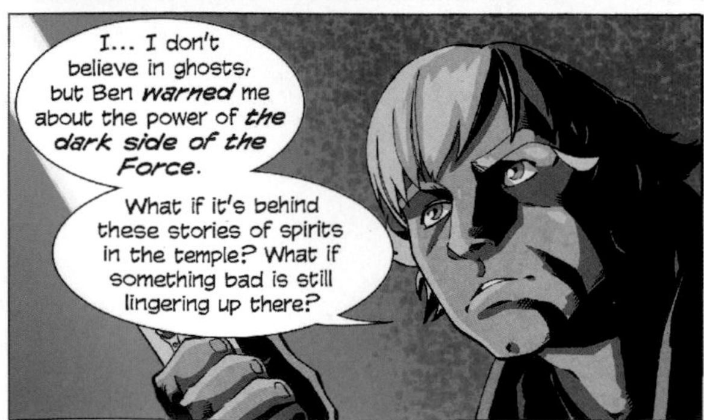
I... I don't believe in ghosts, but Ben *warned* me about the power of *the dark side of the Force*.
What if it's behind these stories of spirits in the temple? What if something bad is still lingering up there?

Let's find out!
Breet! Breet! Vooda-doop!

WHOOOP! WHOOOP! BOODA-DOOP!
Keep your voice *down*, Artoo! *Please!* These passages look as though they might *collapse* at the *slightest* sound!
Can you imagine being entombed in this dreadful place for millennia without power while vermin nibbled at your wiring?

Master Luke, you're facing our predicament with admirable calm, I must say.
It's *the Force*, Threepio. I can feel it getting stronger.
Stronger, or perhaps I'm feeling a deeper connection with it.

Blast! Looks like the passage is blocked.
Oh, no, a cave-in! Didn't I *tell* you, Artoo?
It's obviously *completely* impassable.

I suppose we'll have to go back to Tikaroo.
No, it's mostly loose stone. I can feel fresh air, in fact.
Come and help me clear this stuff out of the way.

But, Master Luke, I'm not programmed for *demolition*.

Never mind. The rocks are giving way on the other side. We're almost through...
WEEEP! VOOTA-DOOP!

We're here! We're in the ruins of Eedit!
This is the place I saw in my dream!
They tried to erase everything here that was beautiful.
But they've failed.
Pikhrons!
They must feel safe here. They know the hunters don't come inside the perimeter.

Watch yourself, Threepio!
Ooh!
That's an *impact crater*. Looks like *Imperial bombers* have opened up these pits *all over* the place.
There's blast marks all over these statues too.
The Empire wanted to *destroy* this place.
Luke...
This place is strong with the Force.
Ben?
Here you will learn to open yourself to it, to guide its possibilities, obey its commands...

And to pass its *tests*.
May the Force be with you, Luke.
Master Luke, we've found something!

Vreeep!
Oh, very well, *you* found it.

Artoo has found what appears to be a *lever* at the top of this pillar.

I have no idea what a switch might be doing all the way up *there*.
Well, unless the Jedi who lived here were very tall...

Then I'm guessing it was designed to be moved using *the Force*.

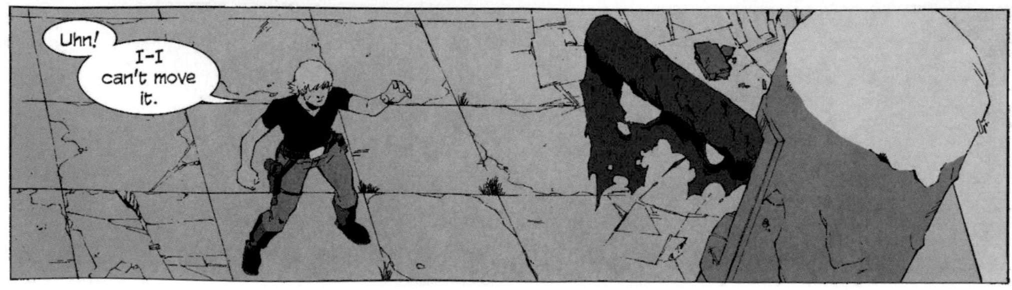
Uhn!
I-I can't move it.

WEOO-REEEP!
No, Artoo. I'm going to stay here and move that lever! *That's* why I'm here, to learn how to use the Force!
I'm going to try again...

"...And I'm going to *keep* trying...

"...I'll stay out here all night if I have to!"

Still nothing!

I just can't seem to do it.
I don't understand *how* to do it, and there's no one to *teach* me.

And there never *will* be.
I'm the *last* of the Jedi!

Meanwhile, in the valley outside the ruins.

Looks like *the Scavenger's* not heading back to Tikaroo any time soon.

He's been waiting down there for *hours*, ever since Luke disappeared into that cave in the wall.
And we know *why* he's waiting, don't we?
Murrhhm?

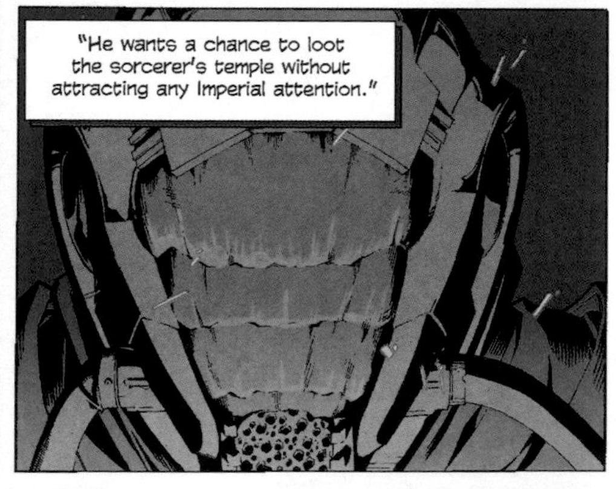
"He wants a chance to loot the sorcerer's temple without attracting any Imperial attention."

Luke might know how to handle that laser sword of his, but it won't be enough to dissuade someone like the Scavenger from getting what he wants.
Dad's not gonna be happy, but I think I need stay out here a while longer. For Luke's sake.

The next day.
OW!
Wake up, Artoo! We're under attack!

Relax, Threepio.
I just lost my temper, kicked a stone that was too big for my foot.

WOOOT?
I'm *fine*, Artoo. Just *frustrated*.

I've been up for the last *hour* trying to move that stupid lever.
Still nothing.

I just-- *hey!*
I'm not a flower. Buzz off.

To harness the Force, you must first feel it *everywhere*.

I... I remember, Ben...
I remember you once told me that *every* life is a vessel of the Force.

I just need to feel that life in *everything* around me...

"...Let it wash over me until I can feel myself flowing through its currents."

I can... I can *feel* the shape of the pillar. I can sense it through the life around it, every microscopic thing living in the stone.
I can feel it all the way up to the lever...

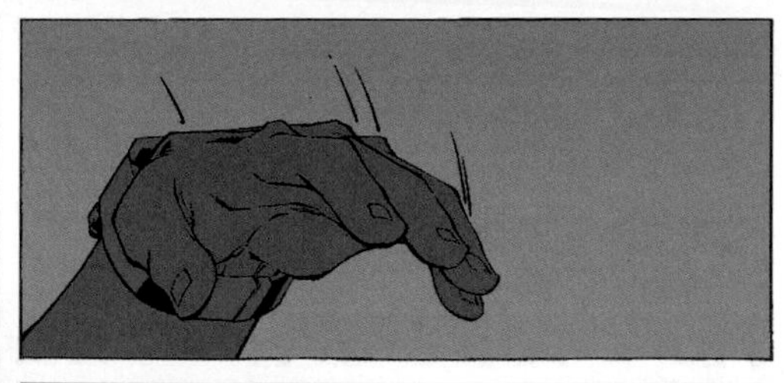

CLUNK!

Master Luke, the lever appears to have opened some kind of *secret compartment*.
And it's full of *training remotes!* Just like the ones I saw in my *dream!*

They look pretty old.
You think we can get any of these things working, Artoo?
WEEEP! WEEEP! WEE-OO!

Thanks, buddy.
That makes *three*. The rest are damaged.

Master Luke, are you *sure* this is a good idea?

I'll risk it.
WOOOOP!

It's okay, Artoo.
Just give them a minute to get their bearings, let their programs kick in.
PSSH!
PSSH!

Looks like those two are leaving.

Which means I'll be training *one-on-one* for now.

The *lightsaber* disciplines the mind, Luke.

It schools the body and spirit.
PSSSHHHEW!

Mind what you have learned.
WOOOOM!

Let the lightsaber be your focus!

Be careful, Master Luke.
PSSH!
It's sizing me up, gauging what I can do.

I just need to feel the Force.
It'll give me all the reflexes I need to guide the blade where it needs to be.

I forgot how *fast* these things are!
VAM!
VWWOOOOM!
KSSSH!

Those attacks forced me into the first and second defensive postures that Ben taught me.
The remote wants to see how much I've *learned*.

PSSH!
Now it's pushing me into the *third* posture!

Whoah!
I need to mark the position of these *pits*. It wouldn't do to fall down there.

SKEOW!
Uhn!

Excellent, Master Luke.
WEEET! WEEET!

Not really, Threepio. I should have *deflected* that bolt. I got *lucky*.

WSSH!
Which means now it's going to attack *for real!*

KSSH! KKSSSH!
VWOOOM!

Ahh!
SKEOW!

Artoo! That dreadful machine has injured Master Luke!
Uhn!
Don't get angry. Just remember what Ben taught you.

He said a Jedi must learn to let go of their anger before calling on the Force.

You must also let go of fear. Fear leads to anger, inviting the dark side in.

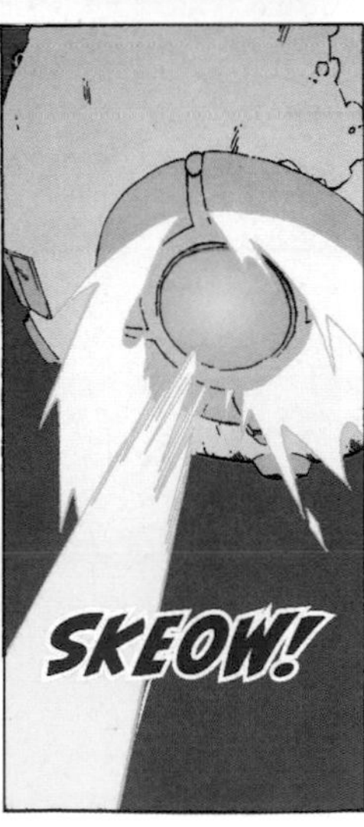
SKEOW!

KKSSH!
VOOOP!
Pcheoww!
VREEEEET!
I'm not afraid.
I won't fail.
Well done, Master Luke! A most impressive display!
Thanks, guys.
WHOOP! WHOOOP!
WSSH!
PSSH!
Oh!
Two remotes! Already? Okay.
PSSH!
WSSH!
As Han might say, "here's where the fun begins..."

Hours later, in the valley outside.
He's building another fire. He's going to wait out here *another* night.
What is Luke *doing* in that place that's so important?

I can't afford to stay and find out. I'm out of food and I didn't bring enough supplies.
What am I even *doing* out here?
Be-Beep!

Great! Another message from *Dad*.
Dad needs me to come home. He'll know what to do.

He'll be angry for sure, but he'll know the best way to help Luke.
MUUURGH!

Sssh! I know you're hungry. But the sooner we get back to Dad's repair shop the sooner I can feed you.
So let's go.

KSSH!
Uhn!

ARGH!

OW!

Ignore the pain. You can *do* this.
Ben taught you the basics when you were on the *Falcon*. Since then you've practiced the footwork more times than you can count.
Forget fear, anger. Just draw on *the Force*.

VOOOOOOM!
KRRSSSH!

KTCHEOOW!

KZZASSH!

About time you had a taste of your own medicine, you dreadful little things!
That's... That's enough for today...

...I'm sure... there's... plenty more trouble waiting for me... tomorrow.
"We're looking for a suspected fugitive from Imperial justice..."

And you said you had *nothing* to report, *Master Kivas*...
I'm just trying to make a *living*.
I was keeping that starfighter as salvage.
I see. And where did it come from?
The truth, please. It would be a shame to have to take you in for *interrogation*...
I...
Sir, he's in the jungle-- *in the ruins of Eedit!*
The old temple? How do you know?
We found a friend of his!
Farnay!

Morning.
VAM!
VAM!
KSSH!
CHOK!
I detest those dreadful remotes...
WHRRRP!

VAM!
Ahh!
I swear they enjoy inflicting pain!

Threepio!
How... How long since the last time I was hit...?
Six minutes and thirty-three seconds, Master Luke!

BEEDA-BEEDA! BRRREEEEP!
I quite agree with Artoo, Master Luke! You must rest! You're only human after all.

Haven't done... enough... Haven't completed the exercise...
Surely a rest isn't against the rules.
No, probably not!
Ouuh!
VAM!
VAM!

Master Luke! Are you quite sure you're recovered? I'd hate to see you damaged.
I'm *fine*... Uhn...
WAHREEEP?
Really? I'm just not sure why you need to make your training so difficult. Next you'll tell me you have to fight without being able to see!
Being able to see...?
When I was fighting that remote back on the *Falcon*, I had the blast shield of Han's old flight helmet covering my eyes.
But I did it. I stopped the remote without being able to see!
Ben told me that your eyes can deceive you. Don't trust them...
He wanted me to trust the Force *instead*. And I *did!*
That's how I beat the remote on the *Falcon*.
That's how I destroyed the Death Star, by shutting off my targeting computer and letting the Force tell me when to fire.

I thought I came to Eedit to learn how to *guide* the Force.
KZZASH!
KZZOOSH!
I was *wrong!*
I need to let the Force guide *me!*
KZZAH!
Threepio, you're a *genius!*
I *am*...?

Murrr?
Well, I like to think I'm programmed for insights.

Later that day.
Okay, Threepio. How long...?

How long since I was last hit?
KZAK!

Three standard hours, eleven minutes, and forty-three seconds.
WOOOO...

Perhaps you ought to rest now, Master Luke. You must be *perilously* low on charge.
I feel great, but you're probably right.
PSSSHUP!

I wonder what's gotten into the ***pikhrons***. Such ***peculiar*** creatures.
Rrrgh!

I think they sense something, Threepio.
In fact, I think I can sense it too, like ripples in the Force... Like something's about to--

--Whoah!
That wasn't a *remote!*
VREEEEEET!
CHOOM!

Stormtroopers!
Surrender, rebel!
Come and get me!
Oh, no, I'll be captured!
VREEET! WOOOT! WOOOT!
PSSSHHWW!
Can't let them arrest me. They'll figure out who I am and make a symbol of me. The destroyer of the Death Star, brought to justice.
Any worlds that might have joined the Alliance will retreat in fear instead.
And, of course, I'll be executed.
I'd rather avoid that, too.
Drop your weapon...
...Otherwise someone could get hurt.
I brought you here, now let me go!
Farnay!

Let her--
Huh?
Hyperspace scout.

Historian.
Farm boy.
And yet here you are with a Jedi laser sword in your hand, like you mean to use it.
ZZZZOOOSH!

Be quiet!
You're under arrest, both of you!

I don't think so.
CLIK!

...!
Uh?
What was that?
It's an electromagnetic pulse to block their transmissions...
ZZZZSSH!
CHOOM!
CHOOM!
Aah!
Well, Marcus?
Let's see what you're capable of.
SKCHOW!
OOF!
I said, hands *off* me, creep!

Uhn... I'll teach you to lay hands upon an officer of the Empire!

Farnay!

Uggh!

Thanks!
KRONCH!
Uhn!

Thank me by getting yourself and the droids to safety...

...Before all this excitement causes an even worse *stampede!*
MURRRGH!

KZZAKKKK
That's the last of them.

Are you alright, Famay?
I'm *fine*. *Let's* go!
BREET! WOOTA-WOOOT!

Hey! What are you *doing?*

Making it harder for the Empire to figure out what happened here.
C'mon! You can't *trust him!*

This is no business of *yours*, brat!
And you, Marcus. Just what are you? You're no hyperspace scout, that's for sure. And you can use that sorcerer's weapon better than you let on.

Famay's *right*, isn't she?

The Force wasn't warning me about the stormtroopers. It was warning *me* about *you.*
The Force. So you're a *Jedi,* then? I don't think so. You don't have their *skills.* So what *are* you?

What was the word the sorcerers used, before the Empire came for them? "*Padawan,*" that was it. An apprentice.
But what good's an apprentice without a master?

Nobody's Padawan, the last apprentice of an extinct religion.
Care for a duel?

I've been looking for a way into this place for *years*-- and now you've been good enough to find one for me.
And now you know there's *nothing* left for you to *steal.*

KZAKKKK!
That's where you're wrong, Nobody's Padawan.
The Empire bombed the temple, but I believe the vaults and storerooms below are intact.

The Jedi didn't stockpile wealth like that. Uhn!
The only treasures here are what's around you, Scavenger!
You don't know a thing about Jedi--
Omph!

This is an *electrostaff*, Nobody's Padawan. A useful tool and one designed to *kill* Jedi.

It's a pity. In a couple of years you might have passed for a Jedi.
KRZZZSH!

But now you're just a boy with a blade you're not worthy of. A dreamer, Marcus. Pretending to be something you're not.
WHRRRP!

The Force is with me. That's more than you'll ever have.
WHOO-WOOOOM!
Hhn!

Not bad, Nobody's Padawan. Your teacher would praise you...

...If you *had* a teacher.
SCHOOOM!
Aah!
No more games, boy!
KRA-KOOOOOOM!
Aaah!
Master Luke!

You've *blinded* him!
He can't see or hear! It isn't a fair fight!
Uhn!
Who said it would be, droid? Now be quiet and maybe I'll sell you and your little friend instead of pulling you apart.

Such feeble senses--so easily disabled.
Murrgh!

What?
PCHOW!

Get away from him, Scavenger!

Foolish brat.
KZZSH!

You've interfered with me for the last time.
Uggh!

Uhh...
Leave... Leave her alone.

You're a determined one, Marcus.
But it's a little too late for that Force of yours.

I could wait for your sight to return and toy with you a while longer, Nobody's Padawan. But it's time to end this.
Ben?

Argh!
VWOOOOOOM!
SHZZASSSH!
My--Kzzzt! --control box!
RRRMMMMBB!
The pikhrons!
MRRRGGHH!
BBMMMMMRRRR!
Stay back!
Ah!

Luke can you hear me?

The Force brought me here, to *Eedit.*
And what I learned here saved me.

I will become a Jedi. I will rebuild the Order. And one day I will come here again.

I *swear* it on the memory of Obi-Wan Kenobi.
And my father.

"And all the Jedi who once walked these halls."
WHOOOOOM!
Okay, guys.
It's time to go.
THE END.

ART BY **RUAIRÍ COLEMAN** COLORS BY **CHRIS O'HALLORAN**

ART BY RUAIRÍ COLEMAN COLORS BY CHRIS O'HALLORAN

Facebook: **facebook.com/idwpublishing**
Twitter: **@idwpublishing**
YouTube: **youtube.com/idwpublishing**
Instagram: **@idwpublishing**

ISBN: 978-1-68405-874-7 25 24 23 22 1 2 3 4

Series Editor
Elizabeth Brei

Series Assistant Editor
Riley Farmer

Collection Editors
Alonzo Simon and
Zac Boone

Collection Designer
Nathan Widick

LUCASFILM CREDITS

Senior Editor
Robert Simpson

Creative Director
Michael Siglain

Art Director
Troy Alders

Lucasfilm Art Department
Phil Szostak

Story Group
Matt Martin, Pablo Hidalgo, and Emily Shkoukani

Originally published as STAR WARS ADVENTURES: THE WEAPON OF A JEDI issues #1–2.